Mickey's Young Readers Library

This Book Belongs to:

Mickey's Young Readers Library

VOLUME
14
Scrooge's Silly Day

STORY BY JUSTINE KORMAN

Activities by Thoburn Educational Enterprises, Inc.

A BANTAM BOOK

NEW YORK · TORONTO · LONDON · SYDNEY · AUCKLAND

Scrooge's Silly Day   A Bantam Book/September 1990. All rights reserved. © 1990 The Walt Disney Company. Developed by The Walt Disney Company in conjunction with Nancy Hall, Inc. This book may not be reproduced or transmitted in any form or by any means.
ISBN 0–553–05629–8
Published simultaneously in the United States and Canada. Bantam Books are published by Bantam Doubleday Dell Publishing Group, Inc. Its trademark, consisting of the words "Bantam Books" and the portrayal of a rooster, is Registered in U.S. Patent and Trademark Office and in other countries. Marca Registrada. Bantam Books 666 Fifth Avenue, New York, New York 10103.
Printed in the United States of America
0 9 8 7 6 5 4 3 2 1
A Walt Disney BOOK FOR YOUNG READERS

One windy day Scrooge McDuck went to visit
his money bin. Scrooge pushed hard against the
wind as he went toward the bin. He was looking
forward to a whole day of counting his money.

Scrooge shut the door against the roaring wind and entered the money bin. He hummed happily while he counted and stacked his coins and bills.

"Is there a prettier sight in all the world?"
Scrooge wondered as he looked at the neat piles
of money.

Happy that the money was all in order, Scrooge got ready to leave. But he stopped at the large window in the money-bin wall. Through the heavy glass, Scrooge saw leaves blowing wildly in the wind.

"What if the wind breaks the glass and blows all my money away!" Scrooge worried. "What if my money blows all over Duckburg? I can't let that happen. But what can I do to stop it?" he wondered. Scrooge thought and thought. At last he came up with a plan.

Scrooge called his nephew Donald and said, "Come to the money bin right away. It's an emergency! Bring your tools and some wood."

Donald hurried to the money bin, carrying his toolbox and three big pieces of wood. Donald was surprised to find Scrooge standing in a room full of neatly stacked money.

Donald rushed over to Scrooge, dragging the boards over the neat piles of money. Coins and bills tumbled down with each step.

"What's wrong?" Donald asked.

"Oh, no! Look what you've done, Donald. You've messed up my money! That's the very thing I was trying to prevent!" Scrooge said.

Then Scrooge explained to Donald what he
wanted him to do. Donald looked at the window
and shook his head.

"But Uncle Scrooge—this window is made with
very heavy glass. Worrying about the wind breaking
it is the silliest thing I've ever heard!" Donald added.

"Never mind that," Scrooge scolded. "Now you'll
have to restack all that money."

"I will not," Donald said. "It was your silly worrying that caused this."

"Who do you think you're calling silly?" asked Scrooge.

"You!" Donald replied. "Why, I've never heard anything sillier than worrying about things that haven't happened yet! What a waste of time."

"Me? Waste time?! You're the one who ruined my money stacks," Scrooge answered.

They might have argued all day, but Donald had an idea.

"I know. If you can find three people with worries as silly as yours, I'll stack the money. If you can't, you can do it yourself."

"That's fine," Scrooge agreed. "I'm sure I won't have any trouble at all, since my worry wasn't silly to begin with."

So off Scrooge went looking for three people whose worries were sillier than his own.

The first person he met was Daisy Duck. She was busy washing her windows.

"Aren't you afraid it might rain and dirty your windows after you've washed them?" Scrooge asked.

The pretty duck answered wisely, "If I let worry stop me, I'd never get these windows clean."

Scrooge walked on until he found Huey, Dewey, and Louie raking leaves in their yard.

"Aren't you afraid that the wind will blow the leaves all over the lawn again?" Scrooge asked.

Huey shrugged, and continued raking.

"The wind does blow some of them back," Dewey said.

"But we just do the best we can," Louie added.

"This is harder than I thought," Scrooge thought.
He looked high and low through all of Duckburg.
But he only found sensible people going about their
work free of silly worries. Scrooge was about to
give up when he saw someone coming.
"It looks like Gyro," Scrooge said. "But what's
that he's wearing, a giant space suit?"
Scrooge hurried to meet Gyro Gearloose.

"This is my latest invention," Gyro explained. "I'm afraid the world might start spinning too fast, and everyone on Earth will be too dizzy to walk. That's why I'm making an anti-dizzy suit."

"But you can barely lift your feet in that thing," Scrooge pointed out.

"That is a problem," Gyro said. "But I'm working on it."

As Gyro went down the street, Scrooge laughed. "Wearing that funny suit and worrying about Earth spinning too fast is much sillier than my worries about the wind blowing away my money," Scrooge laughed. "I just might win this bet yet!"

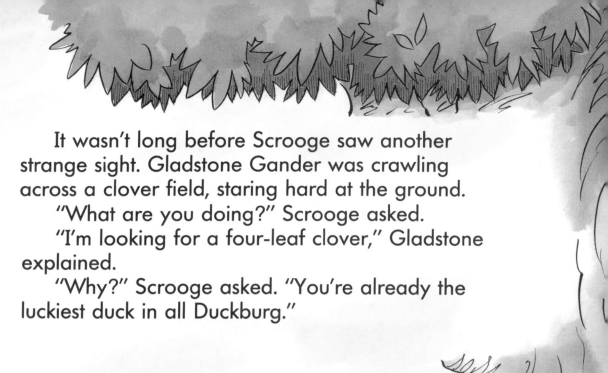

It wasn't long before Scrooge saw another strange sight. Gladstone Gander was crawling across a clover field, staring hard at the ground.

"What are you doing?" Scrooge asked.

"I'm looking for a four-leaf clover," Gladstone explained.

"Why?" Scrooge asked. "You're already the luckiest duck in all Duckburg."

"So far," Gladstone agreed. "But what if I become unlucky? You can never be too sure. I need a good luck charm so that I never lose my luck. That's why I'm looking for a four-leaf clover."

"Have you had any luck finding one?" Scrooge asked. He was trying not to laugh out loud.

"No!" Gladstone said. Then he added, "I'm afraid my luck may have already run out!" And with a worried frown he went back to looking through the clover.

"So far," Gladstone agreed. "But what if I become unlucky? You can never be too sure. I need a good luck charm so that I never lose my luck. That's why I'm looking for a four-leaf clover."

"Have you had any luck finding one?" Scrooge asked. He was trying not to laugh out loud.

"No!" Gladstone said. Then he added, "I'm afraid my luck may have already run out!" And with a worried frown he went back to looking through the clover.

"Two down, one to go," Scrooge chuckled to himself. "Gladstone's worry about losing his luck is certainly sillier than worries about the wind blowing away my money."

"One more silly and Donald will be stacking my money," Scrooge said happily.

Just then, Scrooge passed Gus Goose's house. The tired-looking goose was sitting up in his hammock, looking at the sky. Near the hammock was a plate of cookies, a glass of milk, a book, and a radio.

"What's going on here?" Scrooge wondered. He had a feeling something silly was afoot.

"Good afternoon, Gus. And how are you?"
Scrooge asked.

"I'd be fine, if I could only take my nap," Gus
said between yawns. "But I can't go to sleep. I'm
worried that if I close my eyes it will start to rain.
Then I'll get soaked, and my perfect nap will be
spoiled."

"Why don't you nap inside the house?" Scrooge asked.

Gus shook his head. "It took me all morning to set up this perfect nap. I'd hate to waste all that work. Besides, I'm too tired to move everything back inside. And then, what if I moved inside and it didn't rain after all?"

Scrooge walked away, rubbing his hands together with glee.

"Oh, boy! I can't wait to tell Donald I found my third silly worrier!" Scrooge said.

Then he walked back to the money bin as fast as he could, thinking about the three sillies.

"Gyro was silly to worry that Earth will spin too fast. And Gladstone was even sillier to worry that he, the luckiest duck, would become unlucky. And Gus was silliest of all to worry that the rain might spoil a nap that's already spoiled with worrying." Scrooge said. "It'll feel good to rest my feet while I watch Donald do all the work."

But as he walked, he thought about how silly
he had been. Maybe Donald was right! If Scrooge
hadn't been worried about the wind, the neatly piled
stacks of money would never have been knocked
over in the first place.

"Oh, fiddlesticks!" Scrooge cried. "It's true! I *was*
silly. I'll help Donald stack the money—even if I did
find three people sillier than myself!" he decided.

When Scrooge returned to the money bin,
he told Donald about Gyro, Gladstone, and Gus.
Donald's heart sank when he heard Scrooge's
stories. Slowly he started stacking the money.
Scrooge began to work beside him.

"I won the bet fair and square, mind you,"
Scrooge said gruffly. "But I have to say, you were
right. My own worry was pretty silly, too."

Working together, the two soon had all the money neatly counted and stacked. When they were done, Scrooge exclaimed, "Oh, no! We've got to start over! What if we mixed in some hundred-dollar bills with the one-dollar bills?" Scrooge worried.

Before Donald could say a word, Scrooge laughed. "I'm only teasing you," he said. "Thank you for helping me see how silly it is to worry."

Donald smiled. Then Scrooge added with a wink, "Let's go get two giant sundaes before all the ice cream in Duckburg melts."

Donald and Scrooge laughed the whole way to
the ice-cream store. And to Donald's great surprise,
Scrooge spoke two words he hardly ever used
together: "My treat!"

Think About It

Scrooge's Silly Worry

What was Scrooge's problem? What did Scrooge decide to do about it. Do you think Scrooge's problem was silly? Explain why or why not.

After your child does the activities in this book, refer to the *Young Readers Guide* for the answers to these activities and for additional games, activities, and ideas.

Meet The Sillies

Look at the picture of each character below. For each one, describe the silly thing he did.

What was the silliest thing you ever did?

Fun With Words

Silly Scramble

Scrooge wants to know whether or not you can unscramble the four words listed below. (Hint: Look at the words in the Clue Box to help you.)

YEOMN   ANP

KCUL   YZZDI

Clue Box

MONEY NAP LUCK DIZZY

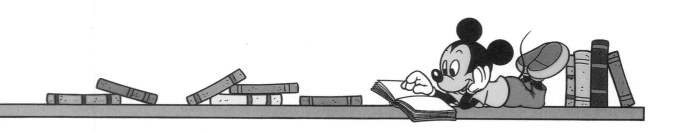

Silly Signs

Look at the four silly signs below. Can you figure out
what makes each one silly?

Mickey's Young Readers Library • Mickey's Young Readers Library • Mickey's Young Readers Library • Mickey's Young Readers Library • Mickey's Young Readers Library